Crazy for
CHOCOLATE

FRIEDA WISHINSKY

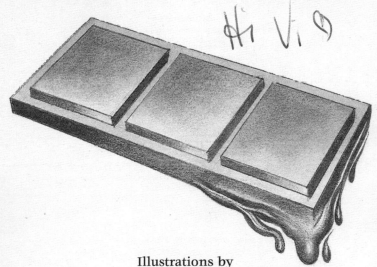

Illustrations by
Jock McRae

Cover art by
Thomas Dannenberg

Scholastic Canada Ltd.

Toronto, New York, London, Sydney, Auckland

Scholastic Canada Ltd.
175 Hillmount Road, Markham, Ontario, Canada
L6C 1Z7

Scholastic Inc.
555 Broadway, New York, NY 10012, USA

Scholastic Australia Pty Limited
PO Box 579, Gosford, NSW 2250, Australia

Scholastic New Zealand Limited
Private Bag 94407, Greenmount, Auckland,
New Zealand

Scholastic Ltd.
Villiers House, Clarendon Avenue, Leamington Spa,
Warwickshire CV32 5PR, UK

Canadian Cataloguing in Publication Data

Wishinsky, Frieda
Crazy for chocolate

ISBN 0-590-12397-1

I. Title.

PS8595.I834C72 1997   jC813'.53   C97-930795-3

PZ7.W57Cr 1997

7 6 5 4   Printed in Canada   01

CONTENTS

For my friend,
Susan Sermoneta.

1

WHAT DO I LOVE?

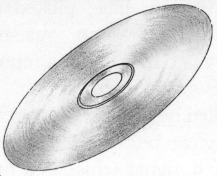

"Choose a subject you love for your project," said Ms Moon.

"Baseball," shouted Robert.

"Cars," yelled Marla.

"Airplanes," announced Nora.

"Dinosaurs," called out David.

What should I choose? What do I love?

Love? Love!

Chocolate!

I love the way it looks. I love the way it feels on my tongue. I love the way it slides down my throat.

I love it in bars, bits, chunks and chips.

Chocolate was the perfect subject for my project.

"Once you have picked a subject," said Ms Moon, "research its history and then write a report."

"History!" I groaned.

"You'd be surprised how exciting history can be," said Ms Moon.

"Yeah, right," whispered my best friend Heidi, behind me.

"Your project is due in two weeks," Ms Moon continued. "Good luck!"

Two weeks! That was ages away, so I didn't think any more about my project. But suddenly it was Friday night, and my project was due on Monday. I only had two days left.

On Saturday morning I raced to the public library. As I opened the door to the children's department, I saw a tall thin lady with straight black hair sitting at our usual librarian's desk.

"I'd like to speak to Mr. Brownstone, please," I told her.

"He's not here today," said the lady.

"Then could you help me find some interesting books on the history of chocolate?"

A strange smile curled up on the new librarian's face.

"Oh," she said. "So you want something *interesting* on *chocolate*. Follow me."

She stood up. A set of heavy keys jangled at her waist. *Jangle, jangle* her keys clanged as she led me to the non-fiction section.

"Here," she said pulling six books off the shelves and dumping them into my arms.

"Thank you," I said, turning to go.

"There's more," she said.

Jangle, jangle went her keys again as she walked to a black desk at the back of the library and unlocked the bottom drawer.

"Take this," she said, pulling a CD-ROM from the drawer. "You'll find it *very* interesting."

I thanked her, checked out the books and CD and raced home. I spread everything out on my floor and started on the books.

I forced myself to concentrate, but it wasn't easy. They were so full of facts, figures, places and weird names that my head spun. I said some of the names out loud: Quetzalcoatl — "Ket-sal-kwat-l." Montezuma — "Mont-a-zu-ma."

I picked up the CD and put it into my computer. This will be more fun, I thought.

A velvety brown chocolate bar appeared on the screen. I could almost taste its rich milky flavour.

"Mmmm. That's more like it!" I said, smacking my lips.

Then a message appeared.

WARNING!
Once you begin,
you must proceed to the finish.
Click once to begin.
Click twice to escape.
WARNING! Keep your mouse
close AT ALL TIMES!

"Give me a break," I said. "I know what to do with a mouse."

I clicked once.

**Your journey has begun.
Good luck!**

Suddenly my hands felt damp — so damp they slid off the keyboard. But it wasn't only my hands. Sweat was pouring down my face.

"Mom! I'm boiling!" I called. "Turn down the heat — please!"

Mom didn't answer. I couldn't wait. "Water! I need water!" I gasped.

I slid off my chair. I had to get to the kitchen, fast.

"Ouch!" I yelled. I had bumped into something hard and knobby. But it wasn't my door.

It was a tree.

2

UGLY WHITE BEANS

I rubbed the lump on my sore head. I wiped the sweat off my hot face.

"I really need a drink of water," I said. But all I saw were trees with giant leaves, squawking parrots and slimy frogs.

Then I saw men cutting football-like things from tree trunks. I ran to one of the men and tapped him on the shoulder.

"Do you have any water?" I asked.

The man handed me a clay jug.

"Thanks," I said, gulping down the water. Immediately the man grabbed the jug back.

"Chop," he said, handing me a

nasty-looking knife and one of the footballs.

"What is this?" I asked.

"A cacao pod," said the man. "Watch."

In one swift chop, the man split the pod in half. Inside lay rows of ugly white cacao beans surrounded by thick white goop.

"Ugh!" I said.

"Here," said the man, handing me another pod. "Chop. Then you can drink again."

I had no choice. I was *so* thirsty. My heart beat fast as I picked up the long knife. Carefully I lifted it above the pod.

"Here goes!" I said. I aimed for the pod's centre. The pod cracked like a melon.

"I did it! I did it!" I shouted.

"Good," said the man, passing me the jug. "Chop more."

I took a long drink of water and

then chopped another pod. As it burst open, one of its white beans hit my nose. I rubbed off the white goop around it. Then I bit into the cacao bean.

I thought I was going to die. It caked my tongue like chalk. I spit it out and bent down for a swig of water.

"Yikes!" I screeched.

A long, fat snake was climbing up my leg. But not my pants leg. My pants were gone.

I was wearing baggy shorts and a loose top.

I sucked in my breath.

"Don't move," I told myself. That was easy. I was too scared to move.

The snake kept climbing higher and higher. It was up to my knees when I remembered the CD's

instructions: **Click to escape.**

But where was my mouse?

"Please. Please be here!" I prayed, as I inched my hand up. And then I stopped. Something lumpy was attached to a sash at my waist. I touched it.

Yahoo! It was my mouse. I clicked once and waited to be whizzed back to my room.

But I was still in the rainforest. The snake was still creeping up my body.

Suddenly I remembered the rest of the instructions: **Click *twice* to escape.**

I clicked twice. And with the last click, the snake disappeared. The rainforest vanished.

But I wasn't back in my room.

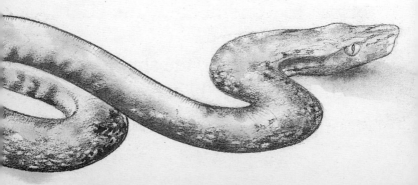

3

WHAT QUEEN?

I stood on a small, wooden sailing ship. A very old-fashioned ship, but sort of familiar. I knew I'd seen it before.

But where?

All of a sudden, the ship lurched to the right and, like an ice-skater,

I slid across the deck. I smashed into a man's chest.

"Excuse me, sir," I said to the man. "But could you tell me where I am?"

"Don't you know?" bellowed the man.

"I'm new to this ship," I said.

"Are you a stowaway?" roared the man.

"I'm not a stowaway," I said. "I don't want to be here. I want to go home."

"We all want to go home to glorious Spain," said the man.

"Not Spain," I said. "Canada."

"Pardon?"

"You know, Canada. North America?" I said.

"A-mer-i-ca?" roared the man again. "What rubbish do you speak? Are you a pirate?"

A pirate?

I looked down at my clothes. My

baggy shorts and top were gone but I wasn't wearing my own clothes. I was wearing brown tights and a long shirt.

"I'm not a pirate," I said. "My name is Anne and I live in Canada."

"We are not headed for any such place," said the man. "We are headed to Spain to tell our glorious queen of the magnificent discoveries we have made."

"What queen?"

"What queen!" roared the man. "The great and glorious Queen Isabella, of course."

"Queen Isabella who ruled Spain and sent Columbus to discover a new route to the Indies in 1492?"

"Ah! So you do know who I am. You've just been having a little joke at my expense. Well, I'll have *no further jokes*, do you hear?"

The man leaned menacingly toward me.

I leaned back and as I did, I was able to read the name of the ship: *Santa Maria.*

"Columbus!" I screamed.

"*Captain* Columbus!" barked the man.

Before I could say anything else, a scar-faced sailor ran over to Columbus carrying a basket.

"What do you want me to do with these beans, Captain?" he asked.

"Let me taste one," Columbus said. "The natives value these beans as much as gems. They say they make a delectable drink."

Columbus picked up a bean. It was a dried cacao bean!

"W-wait C-captain!" I stammered.

It was too late. Columbus bit into the bean.

"Ugh!" he yelled, and spit it right out. "Toss these vile beans overboard! And bring me some water."

"I wouldn't toss those beans if I were you," I said. "Cacao beans make terrific chocolate."

"Chalk!" screeched Columbus, slurping a cup of water. "I have tasted enough of this chalk to last me a lifetime. Be still or we'll toss you overboard with those poisonous beans! And may the sharks devour you all."

Scar-Face began to dump the basket of dried cacao beans overboard.

"No! No!" I cried.

I leaped up and tried to grab the basket. Scar-Face knocked my arm so hard, I went flying. I flew up and over the rail of the ship.

"Heellp!" I screamed as my feet touched the icy waves of the Atlantic.

But just before I went under, I stuck my hand under my shirt and clicked.

Two times. Fast!

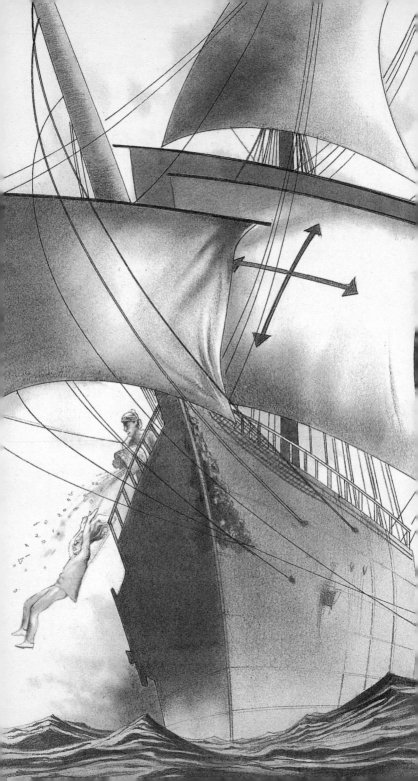

4

NECTAR OF THE GODS

I was standing in a deep valley. Massive pyramid-like buildings with huge steps surrounded me. People surged out of adobe huts shouting, "Quetzalcoatl! The White God is coming!"

Quetzalcoatl?

I knew that name — but from

where? I had no time to think because in an instant, I was swept off with the crowd. As it dragged me along, I glanced down at my clothes. My tights were gone. I was wearing some kind of loose shorts and top again.

I checked my waist. Phew! My mouse was still attached to my sash.

Suddenly the crowd stopped at a large open space. They bowed to a bearded man in armour riding a horse. Behind him marched other bearded men.

Then a man stepped forward from the crowd. He was covered in glittering jewels and feathers. He bowed to the man on the horse and said, "Welcome, O Great White God, Quetzalcoatl! The Emperor Montezuma and his people welcome you!"

Quetzalcoatl! Montezuma! Now

I knew where I'd heard those names. They were in my chocolate books! Those names meant it was 1519 and I was in Mexico. The bearded man was the Spanish explorer, Hernando Cortés, and the man with the jewels and feathers was Emperor Montezuma of the Aztecs!

"Drink," said Montezuma to Cortés. "Drink the nectar of the gods."

Foaming goblets of cold liquid were thrust into Cortés's hands. He

sipped. Then he gagged.

"St-rong dr-ink," he sputtered. "Very spicy."

"Cacao," said Montezuma. In a flash he downed five foaming goblets of the cacao drink without gagging once.

Cortés's mouth hung open. So did mine. How could anyone drink so much spicy stuff so fast?

Montezuma was amazing! I had to tell him not to trust Cortés. I had to warn him that if he did, he and the Aztecs would be slaughtered like chickens. Slowly I wiggled my way to the front of the crowd near Montezuma.

"Excuse me, Your Emperorship," I said, "but this man is not a god. He's a greedy explorer named Cortés and he's out to kill you and your people."

The Emperor spun around. His eyes were cold.

"Who dares speak to the Emperor?" he thundered.

"I do," I said.

"Then you shall die," bellowed Montezuma. Immediately two men lifted me off the ground.

"Hey, lay off," I yelled. "I was only trying to help."

But no one cared. They carried me away.

I was angry but I knew I was safe as long as I had my mouse. I reached down to make sure it was there.

Yes! Safely tied to my sash.

Soon we arrived in front of a small adobe hut.

"Tomorrow she will be sacrificed," said the men. "Tomorrow they will rip out her heart."

They began to tie my hands with rope.

Oh no! I thought. If my hands are tied, I won't be able to press my mouse! "Stop! Stop!" I begged.

But the men just laughed.

"Please — I have to . . . I have to . . . I have to scratch my nose," I said.

"Nose!" howled the men, but they released my hands for a minute.

As fast as I could, I clicked myself out of that bloodthirsty place.

5

LOCO FOR COCOA

wasn't home, but I wasn't with those awful Aztecs either.

Heavy perfume hung in the air like a curtain. A lady in a long fancy gown sipped a steaming brown drink from a delicate pink cup.

Quickly I checked my sash for my mouse. But I didn't have a sash. And I wasn't wearing shorts.

I was wearing a fancy gown! High-heeled pointy shoes squeezed my feet. My hair was in ringlets. And I reeked of smelly perfume.

Where was I?

When was it?

And where was my mouse?

I stood up but something lumpy in my shoe made me trip. It was my mouse! I quickly plopped down in a chair and tucked the mouse inside my dress.

Just in time! The door sprung open.

"His Majesty, Louis XIV, King of France," a guard announced.

A man in a huge wig and embroidered clothes charged into the room.

"Oh no!" muttered the lady

beside me. She quickly slid her steaming drink toward me.

"It's you!" said the King, pointing to me. "You finished it!"

"Finished what?" I asked.

"The cocoa," roared the King. "You know that no one but the King is allowed to finish the last of the cocoa. Now I must wait a month for a new shipment from Spain."

"I didn't finish it," I said.

"Liar! Thief!" the King screamed. "Throw her in the dungeon."

Before I could say anything else, two guards with giant swords dragged me away. They tossed me into a dark, dirty, smelly dungeon.

At least I had my mouse. I could leave this horrible dungeon any time I wanted. And if that dark moving thing in the corner was a rat, I wanted to leave right now.

I lifted my gown to pull out my mouse.

But my mouse wasn't there. I searched through all the layers of my clothes. My mouse wasn't anywhere.

I looked through the small grating in the dungeon door. My mouse was outside on the stone floor.

How would I ever get home? How would I ever get out of this disgusting place? Just then, the door of the dungeon creaked open. The lady who'd shoved the cup of cocoa toward me strode in.

"Bow to Queen Marie Thérèse, Princess of Spain and Queen of France," the guards commanded.

I curtsied — sort of.

"Leave us," the Queen ordered the guards.

As soon as they left, the Queen whispered, "I'm sorry, my dear. But I had to give you the cocoa."

"Why?" I asked.

"You see," said the Queen, giggling, "I'm loco for cocoa. I knew finishing it might make my husband, the King, angry but I just had to have the last bit of that heavenly stuff. Anyway I warned him we'd run out. I said, 'It's 1660, dear. It's about time France got its own cocoa plantations.' "

"I see," I said. "So now can I get out of here — please?"

"Oh dear," said the Queen. "I'm afraid I can't let you go."

"Why not? I didn't finish the cocoa."

"But someone has to take the blame, my dear. I certainly can't. I'm the Queen. But if there's anything you'd like before you die, I'll try to get it for you. Perhaps a nice warm glass of milk?"

"What I'd really like is my — um — the little metal box that's right outside the door," I said. "It fell out of my hands. My parents gave it to me and I'd really like to have it back."

"Then you shall, right away," she said. "And when dear King Louis calms down, I'll even try to persuade him not to execute you."

"Thanks," I said. "But first — the box, please."

The Queen ordered the guards to open the door. Then she picked up the mouse herself and gave it to me. The last thing I saw as I clicked out of that dungeon was the Queen's stunned expression.

That, and the rat nipping at her dress.

6

A CHOCOLATE MOUSE

The sound was deafening but the smell was familiar.

Machines were grinding and groaning. They were mixing a dark thick paste that smelled rich and delicious — like chocolate!

I was in a chocolate factory! I looked down at my clothes. My fancy gown was gone. My pointy shoes were gone. I was wearing pajama-like pants, with ruffles at the ankles, under a wide skirt. I had on a frilly blouse with ruffles at the cuffs. And I had a bonnet on my head.

I was glad my friends weren't around because I was sure I looked dopey. And where was my mouse?

I jiggled my shoes. Not there. I checked my waist. Nothing there. I looked up one of my sleeves. No mouse in there. I looked up the other sleeve.

Hurrah! It was there! My beautiful mouse! This time I would be careful. I couldn't let it out of my sight for a minute.

I looked around the room. There was a newspaper on a table. It was dated March, 1848. A sign on the wall said: FRY AND SONS, ENGLAND.

"Excuse me," said a friendly voice. "I'm Mr. Fry. May I help you?"

"Is this your chocolate factory?" I asked.

"Yes!" said Mr. Fry, beaming. "It's where we make our own invention — bars of eating chocolate!"

"That's great," I said. "Your chocolate looks scrumptious."

"It's the cocoa butter," said Mr. Fry proudly. He handed me a spoon. "Have a bit of a taste," he offered.

"Oh, thank you," I said. "I love chocolate. And I haven't eaten anything in ages."

I leaned over a huge pool of dark rich chocolate floating in a giant vat. I dipped the spoon into the vat. And then — plop! My mouse slid out of my sleeve and sunk like an anchor.

"Yikes!" I screamed.

"What happened?" asked Mr. Fry.

"I dropped something in."

"Quick, Sam!" called Mr. Fry. "Get the strainer. There's something in the vat!"

Sam strained and strained but nothing came up.

I stared into the thick chocolate.

What if my mouse was lost?

But suddenly Sam smiled.

"I've got it!" he exclaimed.

"My mouse! My mouse!" I cried. "Oh, thank you. Thank you!"

"A mouse!" yelled Mr. Fry. "You dropped a filthy mouse into my beautiful chocolate!"

"Not an animal mouse," I tried to explain.

But Mr. Fry and Sam were too busy dumping all the chocolate out of the vat to listen.

"Get out of my factory," said Mr. Fry, "and take your disgusting mouse with you!"

"I really am sorry," I said, picking up my chocolate-covered mouse.

I walked outside. I shivered. It was raining and cold. Oh, how I missed my home — my friends — my mom — my dad.

"Mouse — please take me home," I said, hoping against hope it would. Then I clicked twice.

Nothing happened. Was the mouse jammed? What if it didn't work any more?

I tapped the mouse on the steps. I rubbed it against my pants. Some sticky bits of chocolate fell off.

"Please. Please," I prayed.

I clicked again. And again.

7

NOT JUST ANY CAKE

The mouse had not taken me home.

I was standing on a street beside a fancy café. Chocolate smells drifted out of the shop. The smells made me very hungry. If only I had money to buy a cake and a drink.

Maybe I did. Maybe I'd find a few coins in my clothes. I looked down.

Phew! Those silly pajama pants were gone! The frilly ruffles had vanished. That dumb bonnet was nowhere in sight. I was wearing a long, plain blue skirt — with pockets!

I looked in each pocket. But there was no money in my pockets, just my mouse.

I took a deep breath. That chocolate smelled so good. I walked toward the window of the café and peered at the luscious cakes on display.

Suddenly the door of the café swung open. Two men dashed out screaming and yelling. Each man was holding a silver platter with a dark chocolate cake.

"How dare you bring your torte

into my café!" screamed one of the men.

"How dare you claim that your two-layered torte is the real Sacher torte!" yelled the other man.

"*I* am Eduard Sacher, and my family's torte is the *only* torte that Prince Metternich, Chancellor and Minister of Foreign Affairs of the Austrian Empire, commissioned — not your ridiculous one-layered cake!" said Mr. Sacher.

"Ridiculous?" yelled the other man. "I, Demel, hold in my hand the true Sacher torte: one perfect delectable layer."

Both tortes looked scrumptious to me. I couldn't see what all the screaming and yelling was about. I looked from Mr. Demel to Mr. Sacher and said, "I think both your tortes are beautiful."

"Who are you?" barked Mr. Sacher.

"What do you know about tortes?" boomed Mr. Demel.

"Not much," I said. "But I think..."

"Who asked you to think?" said Mr. Sacher, glaring at me furiously.

"Go away, girl," said Mr. Demel. "And mind your own business. I have things to settle with this phony torte baker, Sacher."

"Phony!" Mr. Sacher's eyes lit up like a torch. He took a step toward Mr. Demel and aimed his torte at his face.

But Mr. Demel saw the torte coming and ducked. The torte hit me!

Now I love chocolate, but getting hit in the face with a two-layered Sacher torte is . . . not that bad! Once I got over the shock, I licked off the parts of the torte that were still on my face. *Mmmm!*

Once Mr. Sacher got over the shock of not hitting Mr. Demel, he said, "Well, young lady, now that you have tasted the real Sacher torte, tell us what you think of my family's divine creation."

"It's delicious," I said.

No sooner were those words out of my mouth, than Mr. Demel threw his one-layered torte at me.

He hit me right in the face too.

"So now tell me what you think of *my* magnificent torte!" he boomed.

I licked a bit of the second torte.

"Delicious too," I said.

"But which one is better?" hissed Mr. Sacher.

"Yes. Tell us," said Mr. Demel.

"Neither," I said. "They're both good."

Mr. Sacher and Mr. Demel did not like my answer. They screamed and lunged for me.

But before they could touch me, I stuck my hand into my pocket and clicked myself out of there.

8

FROZEN

rrr.

I was frozen from head to toe. A blinding white glare stung my eyes. Everything around me was white.

At least I was wearing a warm furry parka, boots and mittens. A blanket snuggled my legs in the wooden sled in which I was seated. But still it felt as cold as Antarctica.

"Mush!" ordered the bristly-bearded man beside me. Our team of husky dogs lurched swiftly across the ice — so swiftly that I toppled over.

"Heellp!" I yelled. The bearded man grabbed me seconds before I plunged down a deep crack in the ice.

"Thank you," I said, taking a deep icy breath.

"Didn't want to lose a member of our expedition," said my companion.

"What expedition?" I asked.

"The South Pole expedition, of course."

"Oh sure," I laughed.

"You doubt we'll make it?" said the man staring at me with his steely eyes. "You doubt that I, Roald Amundsen, and our Norwegian expedition will beat the English to the Pole?"

"Wow!" I said. "You're Roald Amundsen! Then I'm in the twentieth century!"

"Of course you are," said Mr. Amundsen.

"And you'll reach the Pole for sure," I said.

Mr. Amundsen smiled. "Have a chocolate bar. It will give you energy."

I took it, but for once I wanted

something else more. What I really wanted was to sit in my own warm kitchen eating my mom's hot chicken soup.

"Thanks," I said, and almost cracked a tooth biting into the frozen bar.

Suddenly Mr. Amundsen stood up in the sled. "There it is!" he shouted to the men in the other sleds. "There it is!"

The men cheered. "Hurrah! Hallelujah!"

Mr. Amundsen unfolded a red, blue and white flag.

"Come," he said to me. "Help us plant the flag in the South Pole. Today, December 14, 1911, we have made history!"

As we stuck the Norwegian flag into the ice, I saw the men brush tears from their eyes.

Mr. Amundsen announced, "Tomorrow we'll explore every inch of this glorious pole."

A happy roar rose from the men and barks bellowed from all the dogs. Within minutes, everyone piled back into the sleds.

Everyone except me. There was no way I wanted to explore any more of this freezing pole. There was no way I wanted to hang around in all this bitter cold. There was no way I wanted to be near any of those deadly cracks in the ice.

I wanted to go home.

Maybe my next stop would be home. I closed my eyes and imagined my cozy room, our warm kitchen, my mom, my dad.

Then I clicked.

9

DO I DARE?

I wasn't home. Not my home anyway.

But at least it was warm and cozy. A roaring fire glowed in the fireplace of a big country kitchen.

I checked my clothes. I was wearing a calf-length skirt, a knitted sweater, tie-up shoes and white socks.

I checked my pocket. Yes! There was my mouse.

Suddenly, a woman burst into the kitchen, banged open a cupboard and pulled out a slab of chocolate. Then she plunked down on a wooden chair and stared at the chocolate.

"Do I dare?" she said to herself.

I coughed, and she looked up.

"Oh! Hello there! I'm Ruth Wakefield, and you must be part of the family that just checked in," she said.

"Well . . ." I began.

"So, what do you think?" she interrupted. "Should I add chocolate to my butter cookies?"

"Butter cookies?" I said.

"Oh, come now," she laughed. "You must have heard of The Toll House Inn's famous butter cookies. People say they're the best in Massachusetts. But now, here is my problem. I'm out of nuts. Do I dare add chocolate?"

"Yes!" I said. "Dare!"

"That's just what I thought," said Mrs. Wakefield.

She opened a drawer and pulled out two long, sharp knives. "So, what are we waiting for? Let's chop!"

"We?" I asked.

"Of course. You can chop, can't you?"

"Sure, I can chop." A slab of chocolate should be easy. After all, I had chopped big ugly cacao pods back in the rainforest.

Mrs. Wakefield handed me an apron and I began chopping the chocolate slab into small bits.

"Ouch!" I screamed, as my knife missed the chocolate and grazed my finger.

Mrs. Wakefield grabbed my hand and stuck it under ice-cold water.

"Chocolate in cookies is fine," she said, smiling. "But let's leave out the blood."

We both giggled as she wrapped my finger in a soft cloth bandage.

I was soon fine again and I mixed the chocolate into the batter. Then we dropped small lumps of cookie dough onto a black cookie pan.

"Now the hard part — waiting," said Mrs. Wakefield, as she shoved the cookie pan into the oven. "How about a nice cup of Fry's cocoa to help the time go by."

"Fry's cocoa!" I said. "Why I . . ."

I almost told Mrs. Wakefield about meeting Mr. Fry. But I knew she'd think I was as nutty as a fruit-cake if I did. After all, her wall calendar said it was 1930. That was almost a hundred years after Mr. Fry had invented the chocolate bar.

By the time Mrs. Wakefield and I had finished her delicious cocoa, fifteen minutes had passed.

"Cross your fingers," she said as she carefully opened the oven door.

A glorious smell of butter and chocolate filled the warm kitchen.

"I can't believe it!" said Mrs. Wakefield. "I thought the chocolate would melt into the dough in the oven, but it's stayed in little chunks. Why, I may have invented a brand new cookie!"

"The original Toll House chocolate chip cookies," I said.

"My my my," sighed Mrs. Wakefield. "Well, let's taste one."

They were almost the best chocolate chip cookies I'd ever tasted.

Almost — because my mom made the best.

I missed my mom so much. I

wanted to go home, but who knew when the mouse would take me there?

Who knew if the mouse would ever take me there? Maybe I'd be on chocolate adventures forever.

"Oh," I sighed.

"What's the matter, dear?" asked Mrs. Wakefield.

I couldn't explain.

"I need to leave the room for a minute," I said.

"Washroom's down the hall," said Mrs. Wakefield.

As I left that warm kitchen, I saw Mrs. Wakefield carefully lifting each of her Toll House cookies onto a large white china plate.

Then I crossed my fingers and clicked.

10

A LITTLE TREAT

I was sitting at a white desk. I was sitting on a hard wooden chair. A picture of a house by the sea was on the wall. A bed with a pink and red quilt stood under it.

I was in my room!

I was in my house!

I was wearing my own clothes.

I touched my jeans. Oh, how I'd missed them. Oh, how I'd missed everything!

But how long had I been away? A week? A month? A year?

My parents were probably frantic. My parents had probably called the Missing Persons Bureau. My parents had probably given up.

"Mom! Mom!" I yelled, racing down the stairs. The warm kitchen smelled buttery and chocolatey.

"What's all the yelling?" asked my mom.

"I thought you might be worried," I stammered.

"I wasn't worried. I knew you'd get your project done on time," she said. "But you've been working so hard, I baked you a little treat."

Mom opened the oven door.

"Chocolate chip cookies!" I exclaimed.

"Not exactly," said Mom. "I ran out of chocolate chips but luckily I found this wonderful recipe from the original inventor of Toll House cookies."

"Ruth Wakefield," I interjected.

"You've really done your research," said Mom. "Mrs. Wakefield, as you know, invented chocolate chip cookies by accident. She ran out of nuts for her butter cookies, and used . . ."

"Chocolate chunks," I volunteered.

Mom laughed.

"What a researcher," she said, smiling proudly. "So, since I ran out of chocolate chips, I made my cookies with chocolate chunks, the way Ruth Wakefield did long ago. I hope mine are as good."

"Yours are *always* the best! " I said, hugging my mom.

And they were.

11

MIXED-UP TIME

I ate five of Mom's chocolate chunk cookies and drank two glasses of milk.

Then I raced back to my room and tried to pop the CD out of the computer. But it wouldn't come out. I peered into the slot where I'd stuck it.

There was nothing there. The CD was gone! The computer had sucked it up like a vacuum cleaner.

What was I going to do? What was I going to tell Mr. Brownstone? And worse — that strange librarian?

I couldn't do anything about it now. The library was closed. I might as well finish my project and go to the library on Monday.

But what should I write for my project? I couldn't explain the crazy things that happened. I couldn't describe the scrumptious cocoa, chocolate, cakes and cookies I'd tasted. No one would believe me. They'd think I was crazy!

But I had to write something. Maybe I could put some of what I saw in my report.

So I read my chocolate books again. Then I wrote.

I woke up Monday morning feeling happy and scared. I was happy I'd finished my project but I was scared about going back to the library. How could I tell Mr. Brownstone that I lost the CD? And what if that strange librarian was still there?

What if I had to pay for the CD? What would I tell my mom?

Finally the school bell rang. I shoved my books into my bag and walked slowly to the library. My hands shook as I pushed open the doors to the children's department.

"Hi!" said a familiar voice.

Phew! It was Mr. Brownstone! I took a quick look around. Phew! No other librarian in sight.

"Hi," I said to Mr. Brownstone. "How are you feeling now?"

"Fine," said Mr. Brownstone. "But I haven't been sick."

"So how come that lady took your place on Saturday?"

"No one took my place. I was here on Saturday."

"But when I came around ten o'clock to get books for my chocolate project, you weren't here," I stammered.

"Oh, ten o'clock," said Mr. Brownstone. "Yes. I did have to leave for half an hour, but I locked the library up. How did you get in?"

Suddenly Mr. Brownstone looked worried.

Suddenly I knew I couldn't explain.

"I must have gotten the time mixed up," I muttered. I handed him the books. "I'm sorry about the CD. But you see . . ."

"There's nothing about a CD here in my computer, Anne," said Mr. Brownstone.

"Phew!" I said. I was so relieved, I skipped out of the children's department.

But in the hall, my heart almost stopped. From somewhere came a *jangle, jangle* sound. I turned quickly around. I looked up and down the hall. But no one and nothing was there.

Nothing, that is, except a crushed and yellowed wrapper from an old bar of chocolate.

THE HISTORY OF CHOCOLATE

by Anne Banks

INTRODUCTION

Chocolate comes from cacao beans.

Cacao beans are white and bitter. They grow inside pods shaped like footballs that hang from the trunks of the cacao trees. The trees grow in rainforests where it's hot and damp.

HOW CACAO BEANS
WERE FIRST USED

The Inca and Aztec people of Mexico were the first to use cacao beans. They dried the beans in the sun, crushed them and added spices and vanilla. Then they added cold water and stirred the whole thing up and drank it.

In 1502, when Christopher Columbus went on his fourth trip to the New World, the native people gave him some cacao beans. Columbus did not like the beans. They tasted like chalk! Some people say he gave some beans to King Ferdinand and Queen Isabella of Spain. The King and Queen didn't like the beans either.

But Emperor Montezuma of the Aztecs loved cacao. He drank lots of it from beautiful golden goblets. In 1519, when the Spanish explorer

Hernando Cortés came to Mexico, Montezuma and his people were very excited. They thought Cortés was their god Quetzalcoatl coming back to earth. Montezuma gave Cortés some cacao.

Cortés didn't like it much, but he did like Montezuma's gold and jewels. Soon Cortés and the Spaniards killed Montezuma and took the Aztec's gold, jewels and cacao beans back to Spain.

In Spain someone decided to add sugar to the cacao drink. Someone else decided to serve it hot. Now the Spaniards really liked cacao. The Spaniards liked it so much they kept it a secret for about a hundred years. Then someone snitched. The secret was out! The Spaniards had to share their cacao.

When the Spanish Princess Marie Thérèse married King Louis XIV of France in 1660, she brought

along cacao. Marie Thérèsè drank so much cacao her teeth turned black.

Soon cacao became popular all over Europe. In England, people called cacao "cocoa" and drank it in Chocolate Houses.

HOW CACAO BEANS BECAME CHOCOLATE

In 1828, a Dutchman named Van Houten invented a machine to squeeze the cocoa butter out of the cacao beans. In 1847, an English company called Fry and Sons made a chocolate bar using the cocoa butter.

More and more people all over Europe started to make chocolate bars. Many famous chocolate makers, such as Philip Suchard and Jean Tobler, were Swiss. One Swiss chocolate maker, Henri Nestlé, invented milk chocolate.

People also began to use chocolate in cakes. One of the most famous cakes was invented by the Sacher family in Vienna, Austria. They called it a Sacher torte and served it in their Hotel Sacher in 1849. Another famous Viennese baker, Mr. Demel, also made a Sacher torte, which made Mr. Sacher's family angry. Years later the two families argued in court over whose torte was the real Sacher torte.

In the twentieth century, people continued to make and eat chocolate. Some people believed that chocolate was not only delicious, but good for you.

Norwegian explorer Roald Amundsen even took chocolate with him on his trip to the South Pole.

PEOPLE FIND NEW WAYS TO USE CHOCOLATE

Soon more and more chocolate products were invented. People made cakes and cookies with chocolate, chocolate brownies and chocolate bars with nuts, caramel and even peanut butter.

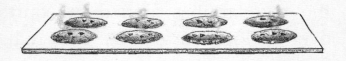

The chocolate chip cookie was invented in Massachusetts in 1930 by Ruth Wakefield. Mrs. Wakefield and her family owned the Toll House Inn and Restaurant. Mrs. Wakefield was famous for her butter cookies. One day she ran out of nuts for her cookies. She had some chocolate in the house and she used it instead. The chunks didn't melt into the cookies, and that's how Ruth Wakefield invented the chocolate chip cookie.

Chocolate is a delicious food. It has made the world a sweeter place.

THE END.

Grade: A
Comments: Well-organized. Good use of resources. Very interesting project, Anne!

— Ms Moon

P.S. How do you know cacao beans taste like chalk? Have you ever tasted a cacao bean?

Frieda Wishinsky is the author of several books, including *Oonga Boonga, Why Can't You Fold Your Pants like David Levine?* and *Jennifer Jones Won't Leave Me Alone.* She wrote this book so that she could combine her love of writing with two of her other loves: history and chocolate!

Frieda Wishinsky lives in Toronto with her family.